l a u r e n   c h i l d

D0239329

# I am TOO absolutely small for school

featuring **Charlie** and **Lola**

ORCHARD BOOKS

for Sofie and her
invisible friend
Søren Lorensen

and for Maisie, Clemmie,

Molly and Ella

Thank you to Goldy

Absolutely

ORCHARD BOOKS, 388 Euston Road,

for taking all the photographs so beautifully

London NW1 3BH. Orchard Books Australia,

17/207 Kent Street, Sydney NSW 2000,

ISBN 978 1 84616 858 7

Orchard Books is a division of Hachette Children's Books, an Hachette UK company.

This edition first published in 2007 First published in 2003 by Orchard Books

Thank you to Simon for his utterly invaluable comments

been asserted by her in accordance with the Copyright, Designs and Patents Act, 1988.

© Lauren Child 2005.

Text and Illustrations

The right of Lauren Child to be identified as the author and illustrator of this work has

for his utterly invaluable comments

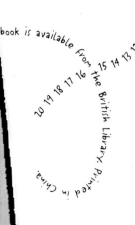

I have this little sister Lola. She is small and very funny.

Now Mum and Dad say she is nearly quite big enough to go to school.

Lola is not so sure.

Charlie

She says,

"I probably do not have time to go to school. I am too extremely busy doing important things at home."

I say,
"At school
you will learn
numbers and how to
count up to one hundred."

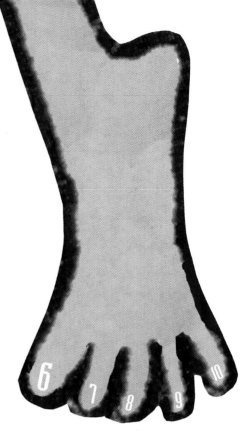

Lola says,
"I don't need to
learn up to one hundred.
I already know up to ten
and that is plenty.

I have ten fingers. And also I have ten toes.

And I 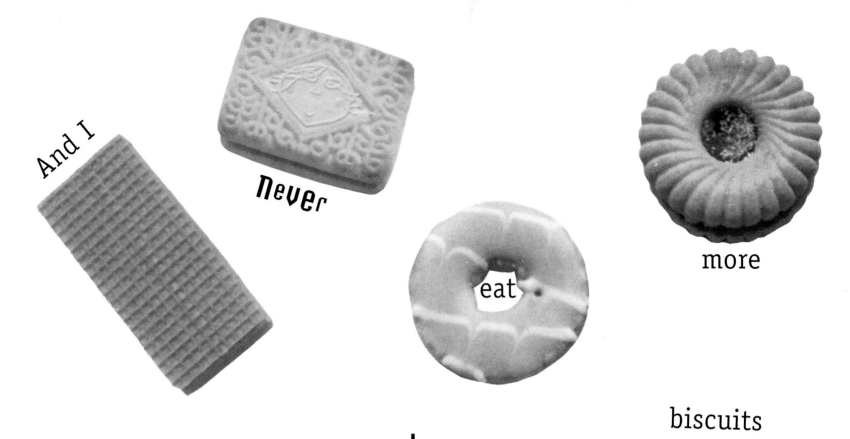 Never

eat

more

than

biscuits

ten

go.

in

 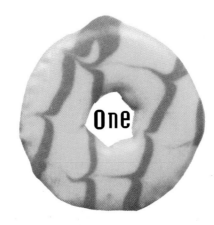 One

Ten is enough."

How would you count up how many treats that would be?"

"Well," says Lola.

"I am not quite sure."

I say,

"And what about learning your

# letters, Lola?

If you know how to write,

you can send cards to

people you like."

"But not everyone has a telephone you know,' Lola," I say.

"Who doesn't?" says Lola.

"Father Christmas," I say. "You have to write him a special note and put it up the chimney to tell

his little helpers your Christmas **wish**. Otherwise the little helpers might get your wish **muddled up."**

"I didn't know that, Charlie," says Lola.

"And Lola," I say,
   "don't you want to
**read words**? Then you will
      be able to **read** your
own **books**. And understand
secret messages written
on the fridge."

   Lola says,
      "I know lots of **secrets**.
I don't need to **read words**,
         and I've got all my
**books** in my head.
      If I can't remember, I
can just make them up."

"But Lola," I say,
"what would you do if there was an ever so angry ogre
who would not go to sleep unless you read him
his favourite bedtime story?"

"I don't know, Charlie,"

says Lola.

Then Lola says,
    "I **would** like to
**read** to an ogre and
    **count up** elephants and
put **notes** up the chimbley.
But I **absolutely** will NOT
    ever wear a **schooliform**.
I do not like wearing the
**same** as other people."

I say,
    "But Lola, you do
not have to wear a
    **school uniform**. At our
school you can wear
    **whatever you like**."

"**Oh**," says Lola.
    "You wait there. I know
**exactly** what I can wear..."

"Well, Lola," I say, "that certainly suits you,

but you **cannot** go to school dressed as a **crocodile**."

Lola says, "This is **not** a **crocodile**, this is a **alligator**."

I say, "You can't really go as an **alligator** either."

"Why not?" says Lola.

Charlie

"I like to wear stripes," says Lola, "but what will I do at lunchtime? You know I will NOT ever never eat a school dinner."

My sister Lola is fussy about food.

I say,
"But Lola, you can take your very own packed lunch in your very own lunch box."

Lola says,
"I do not want to eat at school,
**alone**, all by myself
on my own."

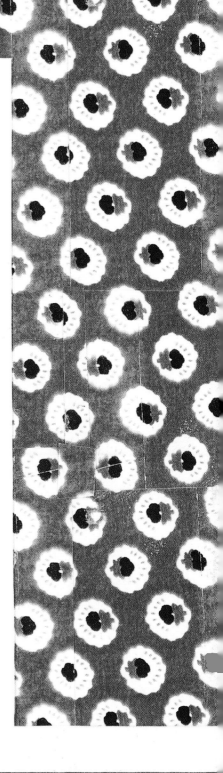

I say, "But Lola, at school you will meet lots of new **friends.** You can have **lunch** with one of them."

Then Lola says, "But I already have **my friend** Soren Lorensen. I would like to have **lunch** at **home** with him."

Soren Lorensen is Lola's invisible friend. No one knows what he looks like.

Walking to school, Lola is all wobbly.

She says, "Soren Lorensen is feeling slightly not very well.

He is worried he will not be able to count numbers, do letters and read words, and no one will

"Lola," I say, "it will be OK.

You'll be fine.

I bet you'll both have a really good time.

And after school we'll have pink milk at home."

talk to him so he will be all by himself on his own."

I can't find her at hometime, she's not by her peg.

But then there she is, and she's not all alone by herself, she's hopping along home with somebody else...

At home, I say,
   "Lola, I **told you** that you would
      have a **good time**."
And Lola says,
   "Oh I know Charlie, I was not
worried. It was Soren Lorensen
      who was nervous, **not me**.
   I was **fine**."